MortaxE
THE SKELETON
WARRIOR

BY ADAM BLADE

ORCHARD

THE ICY F

THE NORTHERN MOUNTAINS

THE

THE FOREST OF FEAR

WESTERN OCEAN

THE

INS
Avantia
TRAL
AINS
GRASSY
PLAINS
KING
HUGO'S
PALACE
THE CITY
ERRINEL
DING RIVER

THE CALM BEFORE
THE STORM

*I*t's been an honour for Silver and I to be with Tom on his Quests – together, we've never failed. We've just arrived at King Hugo's palace, resting before the next challenge. But our enemies do not rest!

Even as we enjoy a kingdom at peace, dark magic gathers. Tom is about to be tested like never before. Can he defeat an evil twice as strong as any other we've met? And will Avantia survive an attack from the six who are meant to protect it?

Only my friend has the answers. He may not be the hero you think he is...

Keep reading, if you think your heart is as strong as mine.

Your friend, Elenna

CHAPTER ONE

A HERO'S RETURN

Tom crossed the floor of his
bedchamber in King Hugo's castle,
pulling at the white ruff of his collar.
He looked at himself in the mirror.
The clothes had been left on the bed,
ready for the King's birthday banquet
in the evening: the flowing red robe,
embroidered with golden thread, was
fastened with a lace collar under his

chin. A servant had asked him to try the outfit on and check it fitted.

"I don't know how anyone can wear this stuff!" he grumbled to himself.

They'd even given him a pair of pointed slippers, sparkling with tiny silver bells that tinkled when he moved. *Please don't let there be dancing!* Tom thought.

He sighed and straightened the robe. This was the price he had to pay for being a guest of the King. He should be honoured, really – King Hugo didn't invite everyone to his birthday celebrations.

Tom glanced at the embossed wooden chest that sat in a corner of the room. It had been many days since he'd last opened the heavy lid. The chest contained his prized possessions – everything he would need on a Beast Quest: his sword, his enchanted shield, and the jewelled belt.

Tom heard footsteps pounding up the stairs outside. There was a hurried knock at the door.

"Tom, let me in. Quickly!"

He recognised Elenna's voice at once.

"Just a moment," he said, unfastening the buttons down the front of his robe and trying to pull off one of his shoes at the same time.

The door flew open.

"Just look what they've done to me!" Elenna raged.

Her face was pale with anger. She wore a yellow dress, shimmering with silk, lace and fine netting. The material was swathed around her

upper body, but the lower half
swelled outwards in a great puff that
cascaded to the floor. A sparkling
tiara sat on top of her head, and the
only sign of the friend he knew so
well was her short, spiky hair. Tom

had to bite his lip to stop himself bursting into laughter.

He stepped aside to give Elenna room as she tried to squeeze herself through the narrow doorway. The dress's folds brushed each side of the frame. Tom tried to disguise his chuckling with a cough.

"I don't know what you think is so funny," said Elenna, grinning as well now. "You look like a conjuror in that outfit."

Tom lifted a foot and shook his toes to make the bells jingle. "No chance of sneaking up on a Beast in these, is there?"

Elenna huffed and tried to pat down her skirts. "You'd think they might have let us off considering the number of times we've saved the kingdom!"

"It's only for one night," said Tom. "And it is the King's birthday."

"I suppose so," grumbled Elenna.

Suddenly, a loud explosion sounded outside. Tom rushed to the window, with Elenna at his side.

"What was that?" he gasped. Was someone attacking the castle?

In the crisp morning air, the palace grounds looked still. There was no smoke, no shouting. Then another explosion. This time a point of red light burst above the turrets of the castle, showering a cascade of rainbow colours.

"Fireworks!" said Tom, feeling his panic seep away.

"Look!" said Elenna, pointing.

Down beneath the light display was Aduro, standing on a patch of bare ground. He was wearing his ceremonial robes – a purple cloak sparkling with silver stars. He took a cylindrical object from a box.

"He must be preparing for the big show after the banquet," Tom said. He opened a window, and leaned out, whistling loudly with two fingers in his mouth. Aduro turned towards them and waved.

But before Aduro could send another firework into the sky, a louder explosion ripped through the air, rattling the window in its casement. Tom felt the rumble through his body. The whole chamber was shaking, and Elenna gripped his arm. "That didn't sound like a firework," she said nervously.

Tom waited for the rumbling to stop. Elenna was right. This was something else. Something bad.

Aduro had turned and was looking towards the west. Tom followed his gaze. Above the western walls, plumes of black smoke were rising into the clear blue sky. The Good Wizard started to run, cloak billowing out behind him. But he wasn't heading towards the explosion.

"He's going towards the stables…" Elenna muttered.

A familiar feeling of dread tightened in Tom's gut.

"Come on," he said "Let's find out what's going on."

Elenna did the same with the tiara. A deep frown was etched across her forehead.

"I'll get changed and meet you downstairs," she said.

Tom nodded as he pulled the red robe over his head. He knelt down beside the wooden chest, unfastened the padlock and flung open the lid. As soon as the sword hilt was in his hand, he felt better. He took out his shield as well.

It looked like he wouldn't be dancing after all.

CHAPTER TWO

ANCIENT HEROES

Tom met Elenna again at the bottom of the stairs. He was still buckling on his sword. His friend had quickly changed into a tunic and leggings, with her bow slung over her shoulder and a quiver of arrows.

Together they hurried across the palace grounds towards the western walls. Servants were standing about in small crowds, whispering to each other. Faces leant out of every window, looking shocked and fearful.

"What's happening?" called a page boy. "Are we being attacked?"

"Stay inside," shouted up a jester, decked in his colourful outfit.

If there was an army marching on King Hugo's castle, Tom knew he'd have to gather the troops. If only his father Taladon were here, but he was away in the kingdom of Rion, checking on Vedra and Krimon, the young dragons Tom had saved from Malvel many Quests ago. *I can do this without my father*, he told himself.

"What do you think it was?" asked Elenna, as they passed a pair of laundry maids rushing the other way.

"I don't know," said Tom. "But from the way he was running, Aduro must have been worried. I've never seen him look so shocked."

The smoke to the west had almost cleared when they caught up with the Good Wizard. He was striding along the track towards the King's stables. Even from here, Tom could hear the whickering of horses, and Silver howling. He hoped his faithful friends were all right.

"Where are we going?" said Tom. "Was the blast outside the walls?"

Aduro looked at him, eyes wide in alarm. "Yes," he said, "but if my suspicions are right, this is the quickest way."

The way to what? Tom wondered.

From the main tower above, King Hugo pushed open a set of shutters and looked down anxiously.

"What is it, Aduro?" he asked.

"You must remain out of sight,

Your Majesty," called up Aduro. "Until we're sure there is no danger."

King Hugo nodded gravely.

Tom didn't understand, but followed Aduro until they reached the stable yard. Apart from the snorting and stamping of the panicked animals, everything looked normal. Storm poked his head over the top of one of the stall doors. Tom stroked his nose as Aduro went to unbolt the main doors. "It's all right, boy. We're here now."

Inside the gloomy stalls, Aduro went straight to a far corner where straw bales were stacked on top of each other. With a few twitches of his fingers, he lifted the bales by magic and threw them aside.

"Look out!" Tom called, as he and Elenna ducked.

He shared a look of concern with his friend. Aduro never normally acted like this...

When the bales were out of the way, Tom approached the wizard's side. Aduro brushed away the last few strands of hay to reveal the wooden boards of a trapdoor.

"I never knew that was there!" said Tom.

"Few people do," said Aduro.

He tapped the trapdoor three times with his staff and it creaked open.

Cold air tickled Tom's skin. He saw rough stone steps leading down to be swallowed up by the darkness.

"What's down there?" asked Elenna.

"These steps lead to the Gallery of Tombs," Aduro explained. "Not many in Avantia know of its existence." Tom must have looked puzzled, because Aduro continued, his voice strained. "The Gallery was here long before the palace, long before me. If I'm right, the explosion was directly above the Gallery itself."

Aduro waved his hand again, and one by one, crystals set into the wall flared alight like stars, casting the stairway in silvery light. The passage went at least four storeys deep.

Tom went to place a foot on the first step, but Aduro laid an arm across his chest.

"This is not your battle, Tom," he said. "I sense dark forces are at play, and there may be dangers greater than any you have faced. Stay here. Let me deal with whatever waits below."

Tom looked at Elenna, who shook

her head. "We're coming with you," he told Aduro. "If it's as bad as you say, you'll need our help."

"I may not be able to protect you," the wizard warned.

"Tom rested his hand on his sword. "Then we'll protect you," he said.

Aduro smiled. "Very well. Follow me." He led the way down the stairs. Silver whined from the open trapdoor, the sound echoing.

"No, boy," said Elenna. "You stay there. We'll be back soon."

Silver sat obediently at the top of the steps.

After they had descended fifty steps, Tom looked back. Beyond Elenna's face, thrown into shadow by the crystal glow, he could no longer see the trapdoor and the stables. He shuddered in the cool air. At the

bottom of the steps, they followed
a narrow passage. Aduro had to stoop
beneath the low ceiling, and thick
cobwebs hung from the mossy walls.
He walked slowly, stopping every so
often and cocking his head to listen.

The tunnel widened, and Tom
made out stone caskets, set upright
into the walls. Aduro continued past
them without comment, but Tom
brushed his fingers over the carved
stone surfaces. There were pictures
of weapons – swords, axes, lances,
shields – and images of men and
women dressed in armour. Words,
etched in letters Tom didn't
recognise, marked the casket lids.

"This place must be hundreds of
years old," Elenna muttered.

Aduro paused and spoke quietly.
"The Gallery of Tombs holds the

burial places of every Master of the
Beasts. And if the Gallery has been
disturbed, then something evil is
afoot. Come."

Some of the carvings were worn
away, others looked newer. One
showed a man with a trimmed beard
and noble bearing. Tom slowed his
steps a little and gasped. The warrior,
whoever he might have been, was
wearing the Golden Armour that

Tom knew all too well. Tom tore his gaze away and hurried after the wizard. *Perhaps my father and I will be buried here too one day*, he thought, his heart swelling with pride.

They reached an archway, and Aduro paused, smelling the air. Tom picked up the scent above the musty scent of decay. Smoke.

Someone's been here recently, he thought. *Someone with a torch.*

Aduro lifted both hands and more magic crystals lit up along the walls, revealing a colossal circular chamber, larger even than King Hugo's throne-room. Tom and Elenna gasped.

More caskets were arranged around the sides, but there were two laid horizontally in the centre that captured Tom's attention. He took a few steps forward and read the letters on the first.

'TANNER, FIRST MASTER OF THE BEASTS'

Tom felt a strange sensation creep over his skin. The figure carved into the surface looked like a boy rather than a man. In one hand he clasped an ancient leather mask. His other hand held a sword. How long ago had Tanner lived? In the silence, he imagined he could feel the eyes of great heroes looking down upon him.

The tomb beside Tanner's was three times as big, and read simply: 'MORTAXE'.

"Who was Mortaxe?" asked Tom.

Aduro's face was creased with worry as they surveyed the chamber. Elenna was reaching up and running her hand over the bottom of a stone plaque set into the wall. It showed a giant scythe. Aduro seemed not to have heard Tom's question. "Odd," he said. "There's no one here."

Tom heard a shuffle in the darkness by the far wall. His eyes picked out a flicker of light.

Whoosh!

A beam of orange light blasted from the shadows towards him.

CHAPTER THREE

MALVEL'S APPRENTICE

Quickly, Tom lifted his shield in front of his face. The bolt crashed into the wood, knocking him backwards onto Tanner's tomb. Blinding light scattered across the chamber, dazzling him and shaking the walls. Cracks snaked across the stone and rubble fell from the roof. Tom heard Elenna scream and turned to see her dive

aside. A massive rock missed her by
a hair's width. Tom scanned the
darkness, trying to catch his breath.
Who did that?

Aduro was down on one knee,
clutching his neck. Tom could see
blood seeping between his fingers.
"Look out!" croaked the wizard.

Another beam of light blasted
through the semi-darkness. As it

hit Aduro, it spread over him like a magic net, pinning him to the ground. He writhed beneath the glowing ropes, but they held him too tight.

Clouds of dust rose from the fallen masonry and the chamber's rumbling ceased. Tom scrambled to his feet, drawing his trusty sword. He pointed his blade in the direction of their hidden attacker.

Elenna rushed towards Aduro, unhooking her bow from her shoulder.

"Let him go!" she shouted. "Whoever you are!"

"Take another step, and I'll snap his bones like twigs," came a girl's sneering voice from the gloomy corner. Tom peered but couldn't see any detail of her.

The beam glowed brighter for a moment, and Aduro cried out in pain.

Elenna pulled up short.

"Do as she says," the wizard called over. "Her magic is strong."

Tom lowered his sword a fraction, but kept his shield up. He peered over the top.

We've walked right into a trap, he realised.

But who was this attacker, with magic powerful enough to harm Aduro?

From the shadows, a silhouette emerged: short and plump, but with a purposeful stride. The crystal light fell over her dark, greasy locks. One of her arms was still extended, fixing Aduro in place. The other was raised towards Tom, threatening to fire

a beam at him at any moment. Her
eyes glowed like burning coals.

"You don't look much like a hero,"
she said. "But then, Malvel always
did call you an annoying little runt."

The name hit Tom like a punch to

the gut, followed by a flood of hot fury. Malvel! So that was who this girl worked for!

"We've defeated Malvel every time he's threatened this kingdom," Elenna shouted.

"She's right," added Tom. "And when I meet him face to face again, I won't back down. Who are you? His latest apprentice?"

The girl giggled, as if Tom had told a joke. "That's right," she said. "My name is Petra, and Malvel has taught me everything he knows. Every wicked spell and evil enchantment."

With her free hand, Petra pointed towards a stone urn on a ledge beside one of the tombs. Before Tom's eyes, it crumbled to dust.

"Together we're going to take over the whole of Avantia," Petra continued. "And nothing, especially not a weak little boy, can stand in our way. This is just the first stage of the plan."

Tom looked on, feeling his anger burn. His grip tightened on his sword hilt. He had to take a risk, otherwise Petra was sure to kill Aduro anyway. But maybe, if he could distract her...

"Stay back," he whispered to Elenna.

"What's that?" snapped Malvel's minion.

"I was just saying," said Tom, "you might need a new plan."

A look of anger crossed Petra's face and Tom charged.

The fury turned to surprise, and Petra lifted her arm to fire a bolt of energy at Tom. He brought up his sword, deflecting the beam into the

wall. He heard splinters of stone
explode behind him.

He ducked the next beam, closing
to ten paces of the evil girl. His plan
was working – she seemed to have
forgotten all about Aduro and
released him from his magical prison.

He smashed away another bolt of
orange light, and closed to within

striking distance of the girl.

But the girl sprang off the ground. She rose through the air and hovered high up in the chamber, looking down at him.

"Foolish boy!" she said. "Did you really think it would be that easy?"

"Come down here and fight, you coward!" Tom shouted.

"Enough games," said Petra, giving a crooked grin. "Time for a real fight."

With one arm once again controlling the net around Aduro, she pointed the other at the centre of the chamber.

A beam fired from her fingers into the large tomb of Mortaxe, flashing like sheet lightning through the chamber and blinding Tom. He felt the chamber tremble once more, and

Tom fought to stay on his feet. As his vision returned, he saw something like molten metal spreading over the tomb's surface, and a sound like an avalanche began to build as cracks snaked across the tomb lid. The stone caved in on itself. Above the rumble, Tom heard Petra muttering words in a language he didn't understand. The light dimmed, and silence reigned.

The jagged edges of the tomb revealed a black space within, but nothing stirred. Tom wondered if the incantation had failed. *Perhaps her magic isn't as good as she thinks.*

"Arise, Mortaxe," Petra whispered.

Something white crept over the edges of the tomb. Five armoured fingers rattled against the stone. It was a hand, almost the length of Tom's shield. The creature gave a mournful groan that seemed to echo in Tom's head. The rest of the body followed, showering earth and small rocks over the chamber floor and Tanner's tomb.

Tom took a step back, fear chilling his blood.

Something evil had arrived.

CHAPTER FOUR

THE SKELETON WARRIOR

Mortaxe was like no Beast Tom had ever encountered. He looked like a human skeleton, but was at least three times the height of the tallest person Tom had ever seen. Beneath his armour, his bones were stained black, as if he had been burned alive.

The skeleton man, still standing half in the tomb, stretched his arms and back, the bones of his spine clicking into place. Jaws full of rotting teeth flexed, opened, then snapped shut. The helmeted skull swivelled round to face Tom, and two dark holes stared where eyes should have been.

Mortaxe climbed nimbly out of the tomb, towering over Tom and his friends. The giant's legs were thick and strong like young saplings. But Tom couldn't tear his eyes away from the monstrous sight of the Beast's chest. Beneath Mortaxe's ribcage was a heart the size of a human head, reddish-brown and dripping blood. It beat rhythmically, contracting and expanding, and stretching the sinews that joined it to the ribs.

Tom looked to Aduro, who strained against the ropes binding him.

"What is it?" Elenna gasped.

Tom shook his head. He couldn't even tell if this creature was dead or alive.

Above, Petra gave a hacking laugh.

"Welcome back, Mortaxe!" she called out. "You're time has come again!"

The Beast turned towards the nearest wall, drew back his fist, and smashed it into the face of a tomb. A slab fell away from the wall, and when Mortaxe withdrew his hand, he held a scythe as tall as Tom, and made from iron. It glittered in the dim light.

The Beast tossed the weapon from one hand to the other, then let out a deadly cackle. Taking two giant steps, Mortaxe planted his feet either side of the tomb marked 'TANNER' and raised his weapon.

Tom felt a surge of outrage. He wasn't going to let this Beast destroy the sacred resting place of the first Master of the Beasts.

As the scythe descended, Tom leapt forwards, swinging his sword. The blow slammed into the blade. Tom's shoulders jarred and all his bones seemed to rattle at once. In a scatter of sparks, the scythe's head buried itself in the ground beside the tomb.

Mortaxe opened his mouth and roared, then twisted the scythe out of the stone floor, hurling Tom aside. Tom could do nothing as he slammed into the wall and fell on his front. He tried to suck a breath into his winded lungs. As his vision cleared he saw that Aduro still lay under the orange bonds, but had managed to free a single arm. Elenna was putting an arrow to her bow.

"The witch!" Tom gasped.

Elenna stretched the bow, brought the taut string to the side of her face, then shot her arrow. The shaft flew across the chamber. Petra jerked aside in the air with a grunt, and the arrow missed by half a pace. But the girl's concentration had been broken. With a fizzing sound, the orange beam that bound Aduro vanished.

The wizard rolled aside, then stood up dizzily. He swayed slightly, but spread his arms. In each palm a ball of light appeared, one green, one blue. Elenna was stringing another arrow. She fired a stream of three shafts at Mortaxe, but they either

rattled off the giant skeleton or passed harmlessly between his ribs. Tom noticed his thick breastbone protecting his fleshy heart.

Aduro sent the blue ball spinning towards Petra, then the green.

Petra met both with orange orbs of her own, and they collided in midair.

"It'll take more than your weapons to defeat me or Mortaxe," she said.

She soared down to the chamber floor and scurried under a large arch on the far side. Tom let her go. There were bigger foes to face now.

Tom charged at Mortaxe again, but the Beast lowered the scythe blade to head height, keeping Tom at bay. Tom bashed it aside with his shield, only to be met with a vicious kick from Mortaxe's foot. He doubled over and rolled aside as the foot thudded down, crunching into the stone floor.

Elenna had run out of arrows and was throwing pieces of rock. They bounced off the skeleton, chipping away tiny pieces of bone and making the Beast bellow and snap his teeth with rage. Tom leapt over a low swipe from the scythe. Mortaxe quickly switched grips and slashed again. This time Tom ducked, and felt

the blade slice through his hair.

That was close! he thought.

He leapt forwards and stabbed at
the Beast's heart, but Mortaxe turned
a fraction and Tom's blade was
caught between his ribs.

"Stand back!" called Aduro.

From the corner of his eye, Tom
saw that the wizard had brought his
hands close together and held a blue

spinning orb. Tom leapt away, pulling
his sword free.

The wizard released the magical orb
towards Mortaxe. The Beast gripped
his scythe in both hands and swept
the ball aside, sending it careering
back towards Aduro. Fragments of
rock exploded from the wall over
the wizard.

Aduro fell beneath rubble, and
Elenna cried out in terror. The

Skeleton Beast's teeth rattled together in something like laughter, then he turned and bounded across the chamber towards the archway through which Petra had fled. His giant form vanished into shadow.

Tom and Elenna ran to Aduro, who was struggling up and shaking his robes free of dust and debris. Apart from the cut to the side of his neck, and the paleness of his skin, he seemed unharmed. Tom turned to go after the Beast, but Aduro gripped his arm with surprising strength.

"Let him go," he said. "For now."

Tom, blood still pumping, sheathed his sword. "What was that thing?"

Aduro sat weakly against the chamber wall, recovering his breath.

"His name is Mortaxe," said the wizard, holding his neck where he was wounded. "He was a brave soldier called Tarik, in the Avantian army nearly four hundred years ago. He fought alongside Tanner, and fell victim not only to his enemy's blade, but to the spell of a dark wizard called Jaitar."

"What happened?" Elenna asked.

Aduro shook his head sadly. "Jaitar cursed Tarik to rise from the grave as a huge armoured Skeleton Warrior called Mortaxe, bound to take out his rage on the kingdom for the rest of time. But Tarik's heart was stronger than the evil wizard. He rose from the grave as a good Beast, loyal to Tanner and the kingdom."

Tom stared across the chamber, to the archway where Mortaxe had disappeared. "That was a good Beast?" he asked.

Aduro struggled to his feet, beginning to look a little stronger. "No," he said. "Mortaxe was a faithful friend of Tanner's for many years. Together, they defeated Krindok, the rabid bull-Beast of the central plains. But what they didn't know was that Jaitar still wanted Mortaxe as his servant. By plunging the cursed heart of the bull-Beast into Mortaxe's body, the Evil Wizard was finally able to control the Skeleton Warrior."

Tom looked at the wreckage of the Beast's tomb, and felt a surge of hope.

"If Mortaxe was good before," he said, "maybe he can be good again."

Aduro stood up slowly, and shook his head.

"I fear not, Tom," he said. "The

curse is an ancient one, and even I do not know the magic to undo it. Mortaxe will be evil until the day he is laid to rest for a second time. For now..." He cast an anguished glance at the doorway leading out of the tomb. "He's roaming free in Avantia."

"That's where we come in," said Elenna.

Aduro gave a weak smile.

"There's something you're not telling us, isn't there?" Tom said.

Aduro's smile vanished. "I should tell you that the ancient books hint at another power which Mortaxe possessed," he said.

"What?" said Tom and Elenna together.

The wizard lowered his voice. "The power to control all good Beasts, and turn them to his evil will."

"That must have been what Petra meant," Tom said. "She spoke about this being only the first stage of her plan."

Aduro nodded. "If the stories are true, Avantia is on the brink of destruction."

CHAPTER FIVE

RACE TO THE PLAINS

Aduro swayed on his feet. The blood had stopped flowing from his neck, but his skin was ashen grey.

"We need to get you back to the castle," said Elenna.

"No!" said Aduro. "There isn't time to waste. My strength is returning and I can transport myself back with a spell. You must go after Mortaxe, and Malvel's apprentice."

"But how?" said Tom. "We don't know where they've gone."

"Yes, you do," said the wizard, pointing a shaky finger at Tanner's tomb. Tom saw something glowing dully on the surface. Tom walked over with Elenna at his side.

Embedded in the stone lid was a plaque beneath the thick coating of dust. He wiped it clear with his hand to reveal a brass panel etched with a map of Avantia. Much of the landscape looked familiar, apart from occasional landmarks that must have disappeared over the centuries. The surface shifted as the shape of a miniature skeleton moved northwest, towards the Central Plains.

"The Great Wizard Nathren created the map," said Aduro. "You must take it with you."

"Are you sure?" Tom asked. He didn't want to damage the ancient grave.

Aduro nodded sombrely. "We must do all we can to defeat this Beast." Tom took out his sword and placed the point in the small crack between the panel and the stone.

"Why is he heading for the Plains?" asked Elenna. "There's nothing there."

"I suppose we'll find out," said Tom, wiggling his sword-tip to loosen the map. It popped free. But as he crouched to gather it up, his shield began to vibrate.

"What's happening?" he muttered.

The shield shook more violently on his arm, as all of the tokens embedded in its surface hummed.

"The Good Beasts of Avantia are on
the move," he said.

A sharp pain flashed across his
temples, and his brain was filled
with the sounds of anguished Beasts.
Bellows, screeches, squawks and

roars filled his skull, growing until Tom fell to his knees and screwed his eyes shut.

"Tom!" said Elenna in alarm. "What's the matter?"

His head felt as though it was about to explode.

"It's the red jewel of Torgor," he gasped, clutching at the jewel in his belt that let him sense the emotions of Beasts. "They're in pain. Something...something terrible is happening to them."

Next Tom heard Aduro's voice close to his ear, and felt a hand on his shoulder.

"Mortaxe's will has touched them already," he said. "Like you, he can summon them to him. It is happening more quickly that we could have imagined. He is turning them violent, reaching into their hearts and filling them with darkness."

The clashing sounds dimmed in Tom's head and the pain began to seep away. He staggered to his feet, rubbing his temples.

"Then we have to go at once," he said. "Are you sure you are all right?" he asked the wizard.

Aduro nodded. "My strength has almost returned," he said. "Go now, and good luck."

Tom tucked the map into his tunic. He and Elenna raced out of the chamber and back along the passage lined with tombs. He took the steps three at a time until they burst out into the stables again. Storm was there, much calmer than before, munching some hay. Tom found the

stallion's saddle, and threw it over
Storm's back. He began to fasten
the buckles.

"You think we should take them
with us?" asked Elenna.

"We need as many friends as
possible on this Quest," he said.

Elenna whistled for Silver. Tom
expected to see him bounding over
the half-height stable door, but at
first he didn't come. His friend

whistled again, and this time Silver padded slowly into the stables. His head was lowered, and he seemed half-asleep.

That's strange, Tom thought. *Normally he's so eager to get going.*

Elenna stroked the thick fur behind his head.

"Avantia needs us again, Silver," said Elenna. "Are you ready?"

Instead of lifting his head and howling, her wolf yawned. Elenna frowned. "What's wrong, boy?"

Tom led Storm out of the stables, placed one foot in the stirrup and swung up into the saddle. He offered a hand to Elenna and she swung up behind him.

Tom checked the map again. It showed Mortaxe had almost reached the centre of the Great Plains. He must have been moving at incredible speed, and Tom shivered as he thought of the giant skeleton bounding across the grasslands.

Is Petra still with him? he wondered.

Storm cantered through the cobbles of the palace grounds, while King Hugo's staff stood aside to watch them pass. As Elenna stopped at the armoury to refill her quiver, a clutch of children stood beside their parents, looking afraid. One waved, and Tom gave him a reassuring smile.

A baker looked on gravely. "Good luck!" he muttered under his breath.

As Tom and Elenna reached the lowering drawbridge, he caught sight of Aduro in the gatehouse above. The wizard bowed his head in farewell, then Storm clattered over the moat.

Tom rode Storm hard around the southern treeline of the Forest of Fear. Silver streaked beside them. Normally Storm didn't need to be pushed into a gallop and Elenna's wolf had always been tireless. But now he could sense them both flagging. The fields that bordered the city spread out ahead of them, rich farm pastures under a blue sky. Cows and sheep grazed happily in the fields. It was hard to believe that evil lurked out there.

Tom leant over to pat Storm's neck,

but as he did so, the blinding pain returned to his head: the six Good Beasts called to him at once, but in tones of fierce anger, pain and hate. Tom's world span and he slumped forward in the saddle.

"Tom!" shouted Elenna. He felt her hands reach around him and take the reins, drawing Storm to a sharp halt. Tom clutched his head, trying to block the pain.

"It's the Beasts again," he said through gritted teeth.

Almost at once, the pain began to lessen, and looking down he realised why. Elenna's hands were scrabbling at his belt, prising the red jewel away.

"No!" he shouted, trying to stop her, but the clamour in his head was too great. A moment later, the jewel was free and the pain vanished like a snuffed-out candle.

Elenna tucked the jewel into her tunic. "We need you to be able to fight, Tom. You can have it back when all this is over."

Shame flushed Tom's cheeks. *Wasn't he meant to be connected to the Beasts? But how could he complete his Quest whilst he was in agony?*

"I know you're right," he said.

Shriek!

The noise came from above. Tom jerked his head towards the sky and gasped. Soaring through the air was a giant bird with bronze talons and a beak of gold.

"It's Epos!" cried Elenna.

Tom felt a rush of relief. The great Flame Bird flapped her tawny wings and screeched again.

Tom called out. "Epos!"

The fiery Beast dipped her beak and stared at him with blazing eyes. She turned into a steep dive, drawing her golden claws up beneath her belly. Only then did Tom see the spark of a fireball growing between them.

"Look out," said Tom. "She's going to attack us!"

CHAPTER SIX

PETRA'S CURSE

Epos hurled the fireball towards them. It streamed like a comet, trailing fire. Tom yanked on Storm's reins to jerk the stallion aside, and the deadly fireball crashed into the grass with a cloud of choking smoke. It rolled past them, baking Tom's face with heat and leaving a trail of flickering fires and blackened grass. Silver wasn't quite quick enough

though, and the tip of his tail caught alight. The wolf howled and rolled, extinguishing the flame.

"What's she doing?" asked Elenna.

Epos swooped low overhead, crying out viciously. Tom saw her eyes blazing with a look he hadn't seen since his first Quests, when Malvel controlled the Good Beasts. It was a look of pure hatred. Tom watched

her fly off towards the centre of
the Plains, disappearing out of sight.

"It looks like Mortaxe has already
used his powers," he said. "Aduro
was right."

If Epos's dark nature was so easily
released, did that mean the other
Good Beasts were now his enemies
too? And if so, how could he possibly
face them all at the same time?

Tom checked the map again, and
saw that Mortaxe had stopped, right
in the centre of the plains. He
showed Elenna.

"He's waiting for us," he said. "Let's
keep going."

They rode on, dropping down onto
the endless plain with its rolling hills
and rocky outcrops. This was the
home of Tagus the Horse-Man. Now
it was a place of danger, and Tom sat

high in the saddle, scanning for any
movement ahead. They hadn't gone
far when they saw shapes
approaching. Tom drew his sword,
fearing the worst, and his grip
tightened when he saw what the
shapes were: a pack of hyenas.
Elenna put an arrow to her bow.
Silver growled and flattened his ears.

But the yapping pack of hyenas veered aside and ran straight past them. Tom caught the flashes of their snapping teeth and drooling lips, but their eyes barely flickered onto him and Elenna.

"They seem scared," said Elenna.

Tom sheathed his sword, nodding grimly. "And if there's one thing we learnt on our Quest with Trillion, it's that hyenas don't scare easily."

It has to be Mortaxe's doing, he thought.

They were nearing the place where the map said Mortaxe had stopped. But there was no sign of the evil Beast. Epos and Ferno were circling each other in the sky. Epos soared on the hot air, barely moving her wings. The dragon's great snaking tail swayed as his scaly wings thrust

him through the air. Flames flickered
in Ferno's mouth.

Tom brought Storm to a halt at
a safe distance.

"I don't like this," Elenna said.
"Where's Mortaxe? It's too quiet."

"It might be a trap," said Tom.

Neither of the flying Beasts came any closer. They seemed intent on circling the same spot above the ground. Tom checked the map again.

"Mortaxe should be here, too," he said, his frustration growing.

Silver took a few steps forward, sniffing the air. His ears lifted, as though listening for danger. Then Storm broke into a slow walk. Tom hadn't even nudged his flanks with his heels.

"The animals seem fine to carry on," said Elenna. "Maybe their instincts are telling them that it's safe."

Tom could hear the uncertainty in his friend's voice, but he let Storm lead them onwards. He eyed the sky cautiously. If he had to, he knew he could gallop out of danger quickly.

Soon they were directly beneath Epos
and Ferno, who hovered in the air,
batting their wings. There wasn't a
flicker of flame from either Beast.

Maybe the spell has been broken, Tom
thought.

Storm stopped abruptly. He and
Silver were suddenly still as statues.

"Silver?" said Elenna.

The wolf didn't turn his head. He
was looking at the horizon, where
two huge figures were bounding over
the plains. Nanook, the snow-white

Beast from the north, and Arcta the
mountain giant, with his shaggy
brown hair. The ground shook as
Tom made out Tagus the Horse Man
galloping closer.

Suddenly, he felt outnumbered.

"Mortaxe has summoned all the
Good Beasts of Avantia," Elenna said.
"But where is he?"

The rumbling under Storm's hooves
grew stronger and Tom realised it

wasn't just the approaching Beasts making the plains shake. It was something beneath the ground. He tried to twist Storm's reins, but the stallion's head didn't turn.

"Come on, boy!" shouted Tom. "We have to get out of here!" He dug his feet into Storm's sides, harder than he usually did. Normally it would have been enough to send Storm into a gallop, but his loyal steed didn't even snort.

"What's wrong with him?" cried Elenna.

Before Tom could answer, a patch of ground ahead gave a deep groan and seemed to crumble in on itself. A crack, shaped like a long arc, opened up. But this was no ordinary earthquake. From the yawning split sprouted a wall of stone.

It grew upwards, blocking out the sun.

Tom gripped Storm's reins tighter. What was happening?

CHAPTER SEVEN

ARENA OF DEATH

In a vast circle all about them, walls
of granite jutted from the earth. The
walls around the outside grew taller,
with colossal arches cut into the
sides. Inside the outer walls, the
ground sprouted stone seats hewn
out of rock. In the centre, a platform
of polished marble erupted from the
earth, with steps leading up from all
four sides.

It's some sort of stage, Tom realised.

"It's an arena!" whispered Elenna.

The structure was immense. Tom doubted whether one of Elenna's arrows would have flown from one end to the other.

The ground was still shifting at the far end of the arena as a huge carved chair, encrusted with clots of earth and snaking roots, emerged. On it sat the figure of Mortaxe, one arm resting along the throne's edge, the other gripping his golden scythe. But there was another change to the evil Beast. He now wore a strange sort of breastplate. It looked like a single piece of leather surrounding his ribs.

That'll make his heart even harder to reach, thought Tom.

"Look, Tom!" Elenna was tugging at his arm, and he turned to where

she was pointing.

The six arches at the side of the
arena were no longer empty. Tom
gasped as he made out five of the
Good Beasts of Avantia taking their
positions. In the sixth archway was
a foul-smelling marsh, bubbling and
smoking. The surface broke as Tom
watched and Sepron pushed his

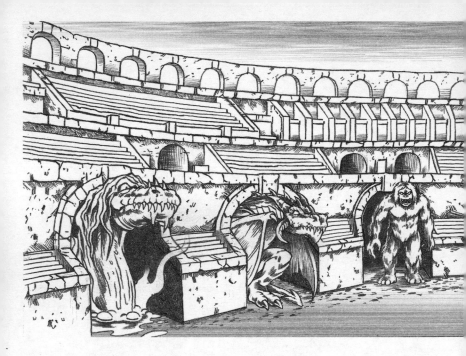

spine-crested blue-green head above
the surface. But the eyes, once pale,
were black with cruelty.

Normally the sight of the six Beasts
together would have filled Tom with
wonder. Now there was only anger.
How dare anyone poison their noble
hearts with evil magic?

Silver and Storm were strangely
silent and still, but Tom could feel
Elenna twisting in the saddle.

"What is this place?" she
whispered.

Tom looked again at the arena, and
the Beasts waiting in their places at
the side. He felt a shudder of horror.

"This place is built for combat," he
said. "Mortaxe is going to make the
Beasts fight!"

The sound of slow clapping echoed
from above. Tom looked up to see
the stocky figure of Petra walking

along one of the arena's uppermost
terraces.

"Well done, Avantians," she giggled.
"Malvel always said you were too
clever for your own good."

Her voice was surprisingly loud,
bouncing off the stone walls. Tom
suppressed the anger that threatened
to overcome him. He wanted nothing

more than to draw his sword and charge at Malvel's apprentice. But she had seven Beasts under her control. He'd have to find another way.

"Your time will come," he promised under his breath.

"Let's get started, shall we?" said Petra.

Tom lifted his shield, expecting one of her orange beams. Instead, she turned away and looked to Mortaxe. The skeleton-Beast lifted his scythe with a creaking sound, and struck the shaft of the weapon three times against the side of the stone throne.

On the third stroke, Storm reared, snorting wildly. Tom did his best to hold on.

"Whoa, boy!" he yelled. "Calm down."

Storm let his wheeling hooves fall,

but bucked straight away, kicking out with his hind legs. This time Elenna's weight fell into Tom and together they were thrown out of the saddle. Tom hit the ground awkwardly, crying out as his leg folded beneath him, sending a surge of pain from his knee.

He rolled onto his front to see Storm trotting towards Mortaxe.

"No, Storm, don't go near him!" he called. Silver went after the stallion. Elenna scrambled, and held out her hands. "Come back!" she called.

Silver turned to face her, his ears pressed flat, tail raised. He snarled at Tom's friend, lips curling back over his sharp teeth. Elenna was open-mouthed in shock as the wolf joined Storm at the foot of Mortaxe's throne.

Tom staggered to his feet, limping as the pain from his knee pulsed up his leg. "They're bewitched, too," he said. "There's nothing we can do until Mortaxe and Petra are beaten."

He drew his sword, and pointed it towards the girl. "You're nothing but a coward, always staying out of harm's way. Maybe you should fight me, one on one. Or let me take on Malvel's Beast."

Petra gave a chilling giggle. "Why not make it interesting? I'd like to see a fight between all the Beasts, wouldn't you?"

Mortaxe stood up from his throne, looming over the arena. He lifted the scythe over his head, whirling it around. Once, twice, three times. Then he slammed the end of the shaft into the ground, sending a tremor across the arena.

The Beasts roared together, blasting anger and hatred. As one, they stepped out of their archways towards the centre of the arena, the ground reverberating with the heavy tread of the Beasts.

Tom's stomach twisted with dread. "She's going to make them fight each other," he said. He lifted his sword. "We have to stop this. Come on, Elenna!"

When his friend didn't respond, Tom looked back over his shoulder.

Elenna's eyes were oddly cold, and her lips curled slowly into a grin. She reached behind her and plucked an arrow from her quiver, stringing it against the bow.

"Why do we always have to do things your way?" she said.

"What's the matter with you?" Tom
asked her.

Her icy gaze didn't shift from his
face, as she brought the arrow up to
point at his chest.

BATTLE OF THE BEASTS

Do you think you can continue?

If Tom were wise, he would surrender. But we all know he won't do that. Tom is marching right into the heart of the battle between Avantia's good Beasts. Marching right to his doom…

This is one fight Tom won't survive – because Avantia's Skeleton Warrior holds more sway over the kingdom's Beasts than he ever will.

Read on – if you, too, are foolishly brave.

Elenna

CHAPTER ONE

BEAST COMBAT

Tom watched as the Beasts closed in. Elenna's arrow was trained towards him and her hand was steady. He put more weight onto his injured knee. It was getting better.

"You won't do it," said Tom. "Not after all we've been through."

Elenna arched her eyebrow. "You're nothing to me," she said.

Tom couldn't believe what she was

saying. Could Mortaxe's magic really be so strong?

"Keep him down there!" yelled Petra.

Elenna's eyes flicked for an instant to Malvel's apprentice. Tom realised he might not get another chance and he charged at Elenna. She released the arrow, but Tom deflected it with his shield and bundled into his friend. She cried out as she fell backwards. Tom couldn't wait to see if she was all right. He had to stop the Beasts from fighting.

He turned and ran towards the Beasts. Storm scraped the ground angrily with his hooves and Silver crouched, growling.

Ferno and Nanook were facing each other, and Tom ran through Nanook's legs, waving his arms wildly at the dragon.

"Stop!" he shouted. "Don't fight!"

Ferno reared back and a jet of fire
shot from his mouth. Tom leapt up
and to one side, narrowly avoiding
being burnt to cinders. Nanook
ducked, lifting an arm as the jet
seared the air. The Snow Beast
bellowed and the smell of burning
fur reached Tom's nostrils. Nanook's
forearm was blackened. Mortaxe's

rattling laughter filled the arena.

"You mustn't!" Tom called.

An arrow whizzed past his head, and he turned to see Elenna. She was readying another shaft.

Nanook stamped towards Ferno, gripping one black wing and yanking the dragon off-balance.

"Don't hurt each other!" Tom called.

His words had no effect. Nanook bellowed with rage, and tossed Ferno spinning across the arena. Ferno righted himself in the air, roaring and flapping his wings to gather himself for another attack.

I should never have let Elenna take the red jewel, Tom realised. *Now I have no chance of reaching the Beasts.*

Nanook grunted and looked down. At his feet, Sepron burst from a pool of slimy water and wrapped his long neck around her leg. He struggled to free himself, but the Sea Serpent held firm, snapping with his jagged teeth.

I've no chance, thought Tom. *Against one Beast maybe, but not six.*

Tagus was thundering to the top of the steps, straight at Tom. He crouched, ready to dive aside, but a shadow fell over him. It was Arcta,

his single eye swivelling madly. He
swatted a tree trunk-like arm,
catching Tom in the stomach. It was
like being charged by a horse, and his
feet left the ground. Tom crashed into
the lower terraces, and thudded
down to the ground. His whole body
felt broken, and he couldn't even
utter a cry of pain. He lay crumpled
on his side, an arm folded awkwardly
beneath him.

The battle between the Beasts continued. Nanook managed to prise Sepron's coils from her leg and lifted it between her clawed fingers. The serpent writhed in her grip, head twisting and snapping, until the snow monster slammed his head into the edge of the auditorium. He thrashed dizzily, half out of the water, and managed to slide back in just as Nanook's hairy foot pounded down.

Tom watched as the Good Beasts of Avantia succumbed to their violent natures. Above the arena, bruised black clouds had rolled in over the blue skies, spiralling and swirling with clashing storms. Jagged forks of lightning split the air, smashing into the edges of the arena and sending up showers of dust and rock splinters. Thunder louder than any

Tom had ever heard cracked against his eardrums. It was as if the very kingdom was tearing itself apart.

Tagus, legs trembling with fatigue, was slapped aside by Arcta. He rolled upright again and turned his attention to Nanook. The Horse-Man charged, battering Nanook with his hooves, driving the Snow Monster backwards. Even one strike would have killed a normal man, but the Beast managed to push back, and wrapped both arms around Tagus's horse body, making him roar.

Tom pulled out his arm from underneath his body, but it was still weak from the impact with the wall. He climbed to his feet, and he switched his sword into his left hand. Elenna had lowered her bow. She was watching the fighting intently.

Nanook had lifted Tagus off the ground. He swung Tagus around, hurling him towards the auditorium, to crash through one of the terraces. She thumped her chest in victory.

She didn't see the fireball that Epos had launched. It smashed into her back, knocking her flat. The smell of singed fur made Tom choke, but Nanook's cries were even worse. Arcta had no mercy for his fellow Beast, though. As Nanook rolled onto her back, trying to put out the flames, the Mountain Giant stepped forwards and delivered a vicious kick into her midriff. Nanook rolled down the steps limply. Tom could see she'd been knocked out, and blood matted the fur around her face.

"That's right!" shouted Elenna. "Kill her!"

There were only three Beasts left: Ferno, Arcta and Epos. Tom stumbled up to Elenna. When he was ten paces away she lifted her bow again, her face twisted with hatred.

"You have to help me!" he said. "I can't do this without you!"

Elenna grinned. "From now on, I help myself," she said. "But let's watch the show first. Better than the King's jesters, don't you think?"

Tom turned hopelessly back to the battle. While the Flame-Bird kept Arcta busy with her fireballs, the Fire Dragon swooped down and raked his jet-black claws across Arcta's back. Blood spattered the arena floor, and Arcta howled in agony. While he was spinning, trying to free himself from the dragon's clutches, Epos attacked his neck with her beak.

The Mountain Giant dropped to
one knee, then fell face down. Epos
and Ferno continued to scratch and
flap until he lay still; the ground
around him was slick with blood.

Mortaxe leant forward on his
throne, his teeth knocking together

in laughter. But worse was seeing
Silver and Storm at the feet of the
Skeleton Warrior. The wolf was
snapping at the stallion's hooves,
and received a kick that sent him
sprawling across the grass.

Ferno and Epos broke away from
Arcta, and climbed high over the
arena. For a moment, Tom thought
they might have had enough, but
then they dived at one another with
screeches of blood-lust. Epos
gathered a fireball, and Ferno opened
his mouth to blast his flames. Epos
darted aside and the jet of fire missed
her wings. She threw her fireball. It
caught Ferno's tail, and Epos raked
more of his feathers out with her
talons. The two Beasts clashed in
the air, hitting each other hard, and
falling in a tangled spiral. They

slammed into the ground and lay still. Clouds of feathers and smoke settled around their injured bodies.

Tom looked at the devastation with anger. Six Beasts were suffering – or might already be taking their last breath. It was time to end this!

CHAPTER TWO

HEART OF DARKNESS

Tom felt a surge of energy through his aching body. It built in his heart and spread across his limbs. Elenna's arrow was still trained on him, but he strode over to the bottom of the terraces where Petra was watching.

"You won't get away with this!" he shouted.

Malvel's apprentice shrugged.

"Me?" she said innocently. "I had nothing to do with this! It's the arena that's to blame. It was built for combat. Violence, destruction and death thrive within these walls. Go on Tom – let your evil side take over, too."

"We're not like you," he shouted at Petra. "We fight to help people. We fight for good."

"Maybe *you* do," Petra laughed. "But I'm not so sure about your friend."

Tom looked helplessly at Elenna, who had put the arrow back in her quiver. Her arms were folded and a wicked light glimmered in her eye.

"I'm impressed that you're not already corrupted," said the witch. "According to Malvel, not many can withstand the evil that runs through

this place. But you can't hold out
forever."

Tom felt the anger burn inside him
again. "Let my friend go." He wanted
to kill this girl, to make her feel pain.
He switched his sword back to his
right hand, and aimed the point at
Malvel's apprentice. He wanted...

Tom caught himself. *That's it!* he
realised. *This is a trap!* He forced his
fury to cool, and watched as Ferno

and Epos untangled themselves, backing off and testing their wings.

"Who do you think will win this time?" Petra giggled. "We can go on all day!"

Ferno roared and Epos replied with an ear-splitting screech. They leapt into the air, meeting again in a blur of flapping wings and slashing claws. The smell of burning flesh and scales filled the arena. Tom realised it wouldn't be long before a Beast was killed. He had to stop them.

He held his sword aloft.

"While there's blood in my veins…"

"Oh, here we go again," said Elenna behind him. "Don't you ever get bored of saying that? Or has the great Tom of Avantia not got anything new to say?"

Tom turned back to his friend. This

person looked just like Elenna, but he knew that beneath the surface, nothing of his old friend remained.

A great thudding made Tom look to the end of the arena. Mortaxe was pounding with the scythe again. This time Epos and Ferno separated, and landed, only paces apart in the centre of the arena. They stared into each other's eyes, pacing slowly but keeping their distance, ready to fight again when the evil Beast gave the signal.

Petra hopped down one of the terraces. "I think it's time for the main event, don't you?" she shouted. "You've escaped one too many times from Malvel's clutches, Tom. But not this time. This arena was built for death, and death there will be."

Tom turned to face the auditorium.

Ferno and Epos backed away to give him room.

"Come and fight me then," he called to Petra.

This made Petra double over with laughter. "Oh, Tom! You really are such a hero, aren't you?"

"Enough talk!" he said.

But Petra's face was suddenly serious. "It won't be me you're fighting," she said, turning towards the throne. Mortaxe hoisted his scythe aloft, and stretched out a bony foot. In half a dozen strides, he had reached the centre of the arena. He towered over Tom, who was only as tall as the top of Mortaxe's thigh.

Mortaxe dragged the scythe's curved blade across the marble surface, throwing up sparks. The red in his eyes showed no pity.

Tom had no doubt this would be
a duel to the death.

CHAPTER THREE

THE INVINCIBLE BEAST

Tom tightened his grip on the hilt
of his sword and held his shield
between himself and Mortaxe. From
the corner of his eye, he saw that the
other Beasts had returned to the
arena. Each had taken its place under
the arches to watch the next battle.
Nanook was bleeding from the side of
her head, her fur matted with blood.

One of the spines on Sepron's back had broken off. Epos and Ferno were last to join the audience.

All the Beasts were injured and panting, but their eyes were on the centre of the arena, greedy for more slaughter. Silver and Storm had calmed down, and waited by Mortaxe's feet. Tom didn't have to turn to know that Elenna had an arrow pointed at his back, ready to shoot if Petra gave the word. He was completely on his own.

If I don't stop this, Avantia will never be the same again.

The sky above Mortaxe darkened as indigo clouds rolled in over the arena. Lightning flashed across the sky, and Mortaxe's spine clicked as he turned his skull upward.

Tom saw his chance, and rushed

forward, hacking with his blade.
He struck the Beast, chipping away
a piece of bone. "You won't win!" he
shouted. "Not while I hold a sword!"

Mortaxe bellowed and swiped with
the scythe. Tom managed to roll
beneath his legs. He tumbled down

the steps. He folded himself up to protect himself, and kept a tight grip on his sword. At the bottom, staggering to his feet, he came face to face with Storm. The stallion rushed at Tom, thrusting with his head. Tom cried out as he was pushed backwards and tripped on the steps.

Bruised and dazed, he climbed back

up. Silver dashed in, snapping with his jaws. Tom backed off up the steps, raising his sword to ward the wolf off, but Silver loped after him, hackles raised.

What can I do? Tom thought. He didn't want to hurt Silver, but the wolf wasn't giving Tom an option. He lifted his foot to push the wolf away, and heard a sound behind him. Tom turned as Mortaxe thrashed with his arm. It struck Tom across the chest, forcing the air from his lungs and knocking him sideways. He slid across the arena and lay still to catch his breath.

Mortaxe peered down at him. A growl emerged from his fleshless jaws. Above, lightning forked from the thick rolling clouds. Thunder drowned out Petra's laughter.

He knows he's winning, Tom thought.

The Skeleton Warrior's scythe flashed down, ready to slice Tom in two. He rolled aside as the blade fell against the stone floor. Tom scrambled up. He could see, through the links of the breastplate, that Mortaxe's heart was thumping faster. He could even hear it, like the sound of a distant war drum.

"You're making him angry!" cackled Petra.

Tom launched himself at the Beast, driving the point of his sword into Mortaxe's knee joint. He twisted the blade and the Skeleton Warrior hissed in pain through his teeth. His leg folded beneath him, but he pulled his weapon free and swung the scythe low, chopping at Tom's legs. Tom managed to get his shield down

in time to block the blow. Around
the edges of the arena, the Beasts of
Avantia roared and screeched their
excitement. The clouds were black
as coal smoke. Tom retreated as
Mortaxe stalked after him.

I have to get close, Tom realised.
Leaping over a swipe from the Beast,

he stabbed at Mortaxe's breastplate. But the leather was tough, and his sword left only ragged gouges across its surface. He tried to get behind the Beast, to hack at his spinal column, but Mortaxe moved as quickly as a cat, turning to face Tom, his joints knocking against each other.

If only I had Elenna to help me, Tom thought. He needed to distract the Beast, and her arrows would be perfect. But risking a look, he saw that she was standing at the edge of the arena, her arrow tracking him as he moved around.

Mortaxe kicked out with a foot, catching Tom's shoulder and spinning him around. Then he felt another blow to the back of his neck and he fell forward, managing to break his fall with his shield, just before his face smashed into the ground.

He heard Epos and Ferno give squawks of approval. Arcta was thumping his massive fist on the ground in time to Mortaxe's pounding heart and Tagus stamped the ground. Tom scrambled down the steps as Mortaxe lunged after him, swishing the scythe in a blur.

"He'll cut you down like corn in the field!" screamed Petra.

Tom needed time to think. He did something he would never normally have considered. He leapt down the remaining steps and ran away from the Beast.

"Coward!" shouted Elenna.

"There's no way out!" screeched Petra.

But Tom wasn't planning to escape. He had a kingdom to save – and its

Beasts. Mortaxe sprang after him, rattling as he landed near the arena's edge. Tom could hear the Beast's heart beating loud enough to come through his chest.

"Come and get me!" he shouted.

The Beast charged, and more lightning flashed overhead. This time it was closer, striking the ground somewhere just outside the arena, and lighting up the arch where Sepron was watching.

As Mortaxe came within range, Tom darted underneath the scythe, and sprinted across to the other side of the arena. Mortaxe turned, his hips clicking, and gave chase. Tom heard his heart beating faster still. When Mortaxe reached him, he did the same again, running out of range and back the way he'd come.

"You can't run away forever!" shouted Petra.

"I'm not planning to," muttered Tom under his breath, rushing past Storm and Silver.

His idea was working. This time when Mortaxe turned to face him, he did so more slowly. He strode, rather than rushed, across the arena, staggering slightly under the weight of the scythe. Tom could hear his heart thumping faster, too.

He's getting tired! Tom realised.

Storm and Silver stood between him and the Beast. With one hand, Mortaxe thrust Storm aside. At the same time, he brutally kicked Silver away. The wolf whined in pain as he rolled into the dust.

Tom felt rage surge through him. The animals might be against him at

the moment, but he wasn't going to
see them being pushed around.

Mortaxe planted his feet firmly on
the ground and raised the scythe in
both hands. Tom copied the action
with his own sword and lunged,
trying to drive his sword-point
through the leather.

138

The blade cut through the first layer, but stopped at the second, grinding against stone. Just what was this armour made of? Mortaxe's teeth rattled with laughter as he shook the sword free. Tom was thrown one way, his trusty sword the other. Now, he only had his shield.

Tom had never felt more alone. All his friends had deserted him. The sound of the Beast's heart, combined with the thunder, was deafening. How could he finish this Quest against a Beast that was already dead?

Of course! Tom thought. *Mortaxe's heart still lived – the part given to him by Malvel. It must be the key to his power.* Tom knew then that he had to find a way to get to the living organ.

But it wouldn't be easy.

CHAPTER FOUR

A DEADLY FRIEND

Tom's sword lay off to one side. He
dodged a scythe swipe, feeling the
blade send a draft over his face, and
ran to retrieve his weapon. He heard
thundering hooves, and Storm
appeared from nowhere. The stallion
reached the sword first and reared
over it. Tom backed away. When
Storm planted his legs again, he was
standing right above the weapon.

Petra giggled from the terraces.

"Looks like you'll have to do without it," she called.

Tom didn't want to hurt the stallion, but there was no choice. If he didn't get his sword back, the kingdom would fall to Malvel and his tribe of evil Beasts. He took the reins and tugged them hard. With a snort of anger, Storm charged at him, but Tom darted aside and snatched up his sword.

Tom lifted his shield as Mortaxe delivered a bone-shaking blow. His shoulder burned with the force of the impact. The Beast seemed to have recovered from his tiring runs across the arena, and came at Tom more fiercely than ever, attacking with both the scythe blade and the long, wooden handle. Tom knew that if he got a direct hit, he'd be knocked out.

Doubts threatened to overwhelm him. Even if he managed to get to the heart and defeat the Beast, Petra was waiting with her magic and Elenna was ready with an arrow. Tom knew how good his friend's aim was.

And what if he managed to dodge both of the girls? Then there would still be six angry Beasts to face. There had to be some way of finding an advantage, however small. He wasn't going to win this fight through brute force alone.

Mortaxe tried to reach at Tom with his long fingers. Tom smacked them aside with the flat of his sword, making the Beast draw back in pain. Then he sprang forward and brought his shield down hard on the Beast's foot. Mortaxe stumbled backwards

into the wall of the arena, shaking off
clouds of dust. But as Tom drew close
for another attack, the Beast whipped
the scythe around and thrust the end
hard into his chest. Tom felt an
explosion of pain but managed to
keep his feet. Now it was his turn to
be driven back, blocking blow after
blow from the scythe.

Tom staggered out of range.
Mortaxe gave his death-rattle laugh.
He seemed to think it was nearly

over. To one side, Tom saw Elenna smiling as she watched along the length of an arrow shaft. *She won't hesitate*, he realised, when Petra gave the word to finish him.

Maybe that's the answer, he thought. *Maybe there is a way to get Elenna's help, even if she doesn't want to give it...*

But first he had to take a risk. Tom pretended to fall, landing heavily on his behind. Mortaxe took the bait and reached out with a bony hand. He gripped Tom around the throat. Tom felt his feet leave the ground as the Beast lifted him easily. He tried to stay calm, but he couldn't help the fear that prickled over his skin. Mortaxe held his arm aloft so all the spectators could see.

Around the edges of the arena, the Beasts stamped their feet, or flapped

their wings. Sepron thrashed his long neck in the water, throwing up spray. Tom heard Silver howl triumphantly, and saw Storm, his black flanks heaving with excitement.

They think it's nearly over, thought Tom. *Let's hope they're wrong.*

"Crush him!" shouted Petra.

Tom felt the cold bones tighten around his throat. He couldn't take his eyes off the empty sockets in the Beast's skull. He didn't have long, if he was going to make his plan work. His eyes fell on his friend with her bow and arrow.

"Elenna!" he shouted. "You always were pathetic!"

Her eyes narrowed and she took an angry step forwards. The arrow didn't waver for a moment.

"You're not looking so heroic

yourself!" she shouted back. "When this is finished, I'll ask Malvel if I can have your body for target practice."

Tom dropped his sword and it clattered to the ground. With his free hands, he managed to loosen the Beast's grip on his neck.

"You always got in the way," he croaked to his friend. "The Quests would have been much easier if you'd just stayed at home."

Tom didn't like lying to his friend, but the situation was desperate. He needed to make her angry.

"I've saved your life more times than I can count," Elenna yelled. "You couldn't survive without me."

Tom half choked and managed to force out a laugh. Mortaxe's grip was strong.

"Saved my life?" he called down.

"All you do is fire those harmless arrows. And you miss, half the time!"

A bolt of lightning lit up the whole arena. Elenna's face went white with rage.

"We'll see how often I miss," hissed Elenna. "It's just a pity you won't be around to marvel at my aim!"

She pulled the bowstring back as far as it would go. The shaft was

aimed right at Tom's chest. He let his body go limp in Mortaxe's iron grip. He needed to conserve his strength.

Tom took a deep breath.

"Go on then!" he shouted at his friend. "Give it your best shot!"

If his plan didn't work, those would be the last words he said.

CHAPTER FIVE

MORTAXE'S WEAKNESS

Elenna released the arrow.

Tom jerked his body upwards, breaking Mortaxe's grip and feeling the shaft swish beneath him. As he fell to the ground, he looked up and saw the arrow buried deep in the Beast's eyesocket.

"Got you!" he shouted, snatching up his sword.

153

Roaring, the Skeleton Warrior staggered, swinging his scythe in aimless arcs. The blade sliced into a section of his chest armour, tearing it apart. Tom gasped as he caught sight of the Beast's dripping, pulsing heart. It was clenching like a fist with each of Mortaxe's furious breaths. Black blood spattered the stone ground like oil.

So the scythe is strong enough to break his armour, even if my sword isn't! Tom realised. *If I can just get my hands on it, perhaps I can use Mortaxe's weapon against him…*

"Finish the boy," shouted Petra.

Around the perimeter of the arena, the other Beasts added their voices to her call. Tom felt their evil cries pounding him.

Her voice seemed to shake the Skeleton Warrior out of his panic. With his other hand, the Beast tugged the shaft free from his eye socket and snapped it. He threw the splintered pieces angrily aside.

"Come here!" shouted Tom, backing against the towering stone wall at the edge of the arena. He knew he was trapping himself in a corner, but his plan depended on Mortaxe coming at him with all his strength. He noticed all the other

Beasts had fallen into silence.

Waiting for the kill, he thought grimly.

Mortaxe took mighty steps, flexing his cracking joints and lifting the scythe high. Behind the damaged breastplate, Tom watched the heart pumping. He sagged back against the wall, pretending he had nothing left. His sword hung limply in his hand. He didn't even raise his shield.

With a rasping cry, the Beast brought the weapon down.

Tom turned aside at the last moment. With a grinding screech, and a shower of sparks, the scythe cut into the stone and lodged there. Mortaxe heaved to pull it free, tugging it from side to side. It was almost out as Tom gripped his sword and turned to the distracted Beast.

"My turn!" he shouted.

With a grunt of effort, Tom hacked
at the Beast's upper arm. His sword
sheared clean through the bone.

Mortaxe's jaws opened in a roar of

anger and pain. He turned his skull
to look at the severed arm still
attached to the embedded scythe,
hanging limply. The Beasts added
a chorus of anguished groans and
screeches.

Tom leapt up at the wooden handle
and pulled it free. The arm bones fell
away and clattered to the ground.

The weapon was heavier than it
looked, and Tom stumbled backwards
before letting the blade clang to the
ground. He had to dodge aside as the
Skeleton Warrior tried to stamp him
down.

"Enough!" screamed Petra from the
terrace. "Kill him, Mortaxe!"

Tom could see the orange glow
building in her palm, ready to throw
in a beam.

"I don't think so..." he muttered

under his breath.

It took all his strength to lift the Beast's weapon again. Gritting his teeth and uttering a battle cry, Tom slashed the scythe across Mortaxe's chest. The curved, glittering blade sliced through the remains of the breastplate, and smashed the ribcage open. A mixture of bone, leather and stone showered over him. The Beast bellowed in agony. He raised his one remaining arm to batter Tom's skull.

Tom dropped the scythe and launched himself up, clambering over Mortaxe's thick thigh bone, and grasping the remains of the Beast's shattered ribcage to heave himself level with the dripping heart. He didn't have any weapons other than his own hands. Swallowing down his sickness, he plunged his

arms into the Skeleton Warrior's
chest.

Tom wrapped his hands around the
heart, and his fingers sank into the
slimy warm flesh. He could feel the
Beast's life-force pumping. Bracing
his legs against the top of Mortaxe's
thighs, and gripping the heart, he
pushed himself backwards, tearing

the organ free.

He slammed into the ground, smeared with gore, while above him, Mortaxe stared down in horror.

The Beast's mouth opened, but no sound came out. Then, his long spinal column collapsed in on itself, and the bones fell apart, clattering into a pile. The skull rested at an angle on top. Any life that had lurked within the deep eye sockets was gone.

"No!" screamed Petra from the terrace. "It can't be!"

Disgusted, Tom threw the cooling heart aside. He tore his eyes from the remains of the Skeleton Warrior, as a shadow fell over him. Nanook stood looking down on him, her lips drawn back over yellow teeth that could crush his bones. Ferno hovered over him, her beak open and fire burning in the back of her throat. Then he saw Arcta, hands flexing, ready to rip him apart, and Sepron rearing his head in a fanged snarl.

Tom tugged one of Mortaxe's arm bones from the pile and held it in front of him like a club.

"I don't want to fight you," he said desperately, even though he knew they might not be able to understand his words.

The other Beasts arrived as well, forming themselves into a semi-circle around Tom. He pushed himself back against the wall. He picked up his sword, but he knew it would only delay the inevitable. Even he couldn't hold off six Beasts.

Above, the sky had begun to clear, and patches of blue had appeared

among the bruised clouds. Epos flew
directly in front of Tom, a fireball
clutched in her talons.

CHAPTER SIX

THE CURSE IS LIFTED

With a screech, Epos hurled the fireball.

But not at Tom. It crashed into the arena wall off to one side, making the whole structure shake. Deep cracks opened up across the stone. The Flame-Bird followed it with a second fireball, creating a gaping hole. Rocks tumbled to the ground.

Tom braced himself for one of the
other Beasts to attack, but one by
one the Good Beasts moved away
from him. Tagus galloped to one of
the archways, and bucked with his
hooves, kicking away great chunks
of stone. Arcta ran shoulder first into
a wall, straining against it. Slowly,
it began to lean. Then, with a huge

crash, it toppled to the ground.

They're destroying the arena! Tom
realised. He couldn't help the smile
that spread across his face.

With her club-like fists, Nanook
pounded at the arches at the arena's
edge, smashing them into pieces.
Mortaxe's spell was broken!

As the dust cleared, Tom saw

Nanook striding over to the other side of the arena, where Petra watched from her high terrace. For once she wasn't giggling.

"What are you doing?" shouted the witch. "Stop that!"

Nanook ignored her. Instead of climbing the terrace, the Snow Monster kicked the wall that supported it. Petra staggered to keep her balance. Nanook lashed out again, making the terrace wobble to one side. Petra gripped the edge in fear. "This can't be happening!"

With a screech, Ferno wheeled in the air to face Petra as well, soaring across the arena on powerful wings.

"Wait!" yelled Petra. "You're supposed to be bad!"

But with Mortaxe dead, Tom could see that Ferno, like the other Good

Beasts, was no longer under the wicked enchantment. His heart flooded with pride to see his old friends returning to normal, their goodness intact. Above Ferno, the black clouds were already rolling away, revealed blue skies beyond.

As the Fire Dragon approached Petra, he arched back his neck, ready to blast her with flames. She pointed at Tom, face livid with rage.

"You haven't seen the last of me!" Petra raged.

Ferno breathed a spurt of fire. But Petra hastily waved her hands and in a cloud of orange smoke, she vanished. Tom looked around, expecting her to reappear at any moment, but she didn't. A gust of wind brushed past him, bringing with it a whisper.

"I will return..."

"Good riddance!" Tom muttered.

His breath caught in his throat as he caught sight of Elenna, lying in a heap on the ground. Silver stood beside her, whining anxiously.

"Elenna!" Tom shouted, sheathing his sword, and breaking into a run.

The remaining walls were ablaze, and the whole arena was filled with a rumbling as the structure weakened, collapsing all about them. Tom had to leap over the fallen sections to reach his friend.

He arrived at her side, and Storm looked on, head bowed and whickering.

Elenna's skin was pale, her eyes closed. Tom struggled to lift her, and made towards a half-collapsed arch. The air was thick with smoke and the cries of the triumphant Beasts.

The whole ground seemed to shake like an earthquake, and the rumbling of stone on stone grew deafening. Tom sucked in acrid breaths as he lumbered out of the arena.

He collapsed across the ground, spilling Elenna on the soft grass. Rolling over, he saw Nanook and Arcta bounding from the wreckage, with Tagus galloping after them. He seemed none the worse for the injuries he'd suffered in Mortaxe's arena.

In the haze of dust and smoke, Epos and Ferno flew over the walls. At a safe distance, Sepron's head emerged from a pool of water. The broken spine on her back was already mended.

With an almighty crash, the last

of the walls folded in on themselves,
burying Mortaxe's bones.

The arena of evil was no more.

CHAPTER SEVEN

BACK TO THE PALACE

Elenna's eyelids flickered, then opened. She focused on Tom's face and frowned. For a moment, he felt afraid. *What if Mortaxe's enchantment hadn't worn off? What if Elenna was still evil?*

"What happened?" Elenna whispered. She pushed herself up on her elbows, and took in the

rubble and rising clouds of dust. "Did we do that?"

Tom smiled. "Sort of," he said. "With a little help from the Good Beasts of Avantia."

Elenna stroked Silver behind his ears. "I don't remember anything," she said. "One minute we were galloping across the plains after Mortaxe, the next… It's all blank!"

Tom stood up and patted Storm

on the flank. "Mortaxe won't be coming back again," he said. "But I think we might see Petra in the future. She escaped."

He offered a hand to his friend, and Elenna took it. He helped her to her feet, but she was rubbing her temples.

"Tom, did we argue? I have this vague memory…"

He shook his head, trying not to smile. Elenna would be devastated if she knew the things she'd said. "I don't know what you're talking about," he said. "When do we ever argue?"

"Well, that's what I thought…" said Elenna, the creases in her brow smoothing. She dipped a hand into the pocket of her tunic and held out the red jewel from Tom's belt. "I'm

sorry I had to look after this for you.
But now that Mortaxe is defeated,
I can give it back to you." Tom smiled
and took the jewel, slotting it back
into his belt. He would be able to
sense what the Beasts were feeling
once more. But as Tom squinted into
the light, he made out a silhouette
approaching. Had Petra returned
already?

   He reached for his sword, but as

the figure came nearer, he relaxed. It was Aduro.

"Greetings, Tom and Elenna," said the Good Wizard. "I knew the kingdom could rely on you both." Storm snorted, and Aduro chuckled. "And your animals too, of course. But listen, Tom, there's no time to rest. You are needed elsewhere, at once!"

Tom was exhausted. Another Quest? Every limb felt like lead, but he squared his shoulders nonetheless. He sucked in a deep breath.

"Whatever it is," he said. "We're ready."

Aduro nodded. "This mission will test everything you have..."

Elenna and Tom shared a look of concern. "Is it Malvel?" she asked.

"I'm afraid it's far worse," said the

wizard, but his sombre features broke into a grin. "The ball starts very soon, and you must find your dancing shoes."

Tom released the breath he'd been holding. Elenna laughed.

"Aren't we excused?" Tom sighed. "It's been a long day!"

Aduro wagged a finger at them. "King Hugo's orders. What would the ball be without Avantia's heroes?"

Tom grinned. "Beasts are one thing, but dancing… Now, that's terrifying!"

"Ready?" said Aduro.

Tom nodded. "If we must."

The wizard muttered a spell under his breath, and the plains disappeared. Tom found himself back in the Gallery of Tombs, standing over Tanner's grave.

"Why have you brought us back

here," said Tom. "We need to go and change if we're to make it to the Ball on time."

"I wanted to show you something first," said the wizard. "Look."

He pointed at the wall of the circular gallery and Tom gasped. In a recess hung the iron scythe, polished to a high shine.

"Mortaxe's remains will never be laid to rest here again," said Aduro. "It's too dangerous. But his weapon is another matter."

Aduro waved an arm, and from a pile of rubble on the ground, rocks flew up, fusing to form a stone tablet. It slotted itself into place over the top of the scythe, hiding it from view.

"It looks as though it was never even disturbed!" said Elenna.

Tom took a last look at the Gallery. So many noble heroes… *One day, I'll be here too*, he thought. *But not until I've completed a lot more Quests*. It was strange to think of his own image carved into stone.

Tom promised himself that he would come down to the tombs again, find out the names of all the buried heroes, learn their brave

exploits and the dangers they had
faced in defending the kingdom. He
could only hope to be as brave as
these others.

"I've transported Storm and Silver
to the stables for a well-earned rest,"
said Aduro, interrupting his thoughts.

"Lucky for some," Tom grumbled.

Elenna grinned. "Aduro, perhaps
you could cast a spell to make Tom
a good dancer."

Aduro shook his head. "Sadly, even
my magic isn't that powerful."

"Hey!" said Tom, laughing. "How
dare…"

Aduro waved his hand and the
Gallery vanished in a flash of white
light. He found himself standing in
his bedchamber. On the bed his robes
were laid out. The silly shoes poked
out beneath. Apart from the cuts and

bruises all over his body, it was like nothing had changed.

There was a knock at the door, and his father Taladon stuck his head into the room.

"You're back from Rion!" Tom said. "How are Vedra and Krimon?"

His father embraced him tightly. "They're growing fast!" he said. "I wouldn't be surprised if they're bigger than Ferno one of these days. How have things been while I was away? All quiet in Avantia?"

Tom grinned, thinking of Ferno lashing the air with his scaly tail, blasting flames at Malvel's apprentice. He thought of how all the Good Beasts of Avantia had proved themselves despite the Evil Wizard's meddling. But he could tell his father about all of that another day.

"A few little problems," he said, shrugging. "Nothing I couldn't handle."

JOIN TOM ON HIS NEXT BEAST QUEST SOON!

Win an exclusive
Beast Quest T-shirt and goody bag!

Tom has battled many fearsome Beasts and we want to know which one is your favourite! Send us a drawing or painting of your favourite Beast and tell us in 30 words why you think it's the best.

Each month we will select **three** winners to receive a Beast Quest T-shirt and goody bag!

Send your entry on a postcard to
BEAST QUEST COMPETITION
Orchard Books, 338 Euston Road, London NW1 3BH.

Australian readers should email:
childrens.books@hachette.com.au

New Zealand readers should write to:
Beast Quest Competition, PO Box 3255, Shortland St, Auckland 1140, NZ or email: childrensbooks@hachette.co.nz

**Don't forget to include your name and address.
Only one entry per child.**

Good luck!

Join the Quest,
Join the Tribe

www.beastquest.co.uk

Have you checked out the Beast Quest website?
It's the place to go for games, downloads, activities,
sneak previews and lots of fun!

You can read all about your favourite Beasts, down-
load free screensavers and desktop wallpapers for
your computer, and even challenge your friends
to a Beast Tournament.

Sign up to the newsletter at www.beastquest.co.uk
to receive exclusive extra content and the oppor-
tunity to enter special members-only competitions.
We'll send you up-to-date info on all the Beast
Quest books, including the next exciting series
which features six brand-new Beasts!

Get 30% off all Beast Quest Books at www.beastquest.co.uk
Enter the code BEAST at the checkout.

Offer valid in UK and ROI, offer expires December 2013

1. Ferno the Fire Dragon
2. Sepron the Sea Serpent
3. Arcta the Mountain Giant
4. Tagus the Horse-Man
5. Nanook the Snow Monster
6. Epos the Flame Bird

Beast Quest:
The Golden Armour
7. Zepha the Monster Squid
8. Claw the Giant Monkey
9. Soltra the Stone Charmer
10. Vipero the Snake Man
11. Arachnid the King of Spiders
12. Trillion the Three-Headed Lion

Beast Quest:
The Dark Realm
13. Torgor the Minotaur
14. Skor the Winged Stallion
15. Narga the Sea Monster
16. Kaymon the Gorgon Hound
17. Tusk the Mighty Mammoth
18. Sting the Scorpion Man

Beast Quest:
The Amulet of Avantia
19. Nixa the Death Bringer
20. Equinus the Spirit Horse
21. Rashouk the Cave Troll
22. Luna the Moon Wolf
23. Blaze the Ice Dragon
24. Stealth the Ghost Panther

Beast Quest:
The Shade of Death
25. Krabb Master of the Sea
26. Hawkite Arrow of the Air
27. Rokk the Walking Mountain
28. Koldo the Arctic Warrior
29. Trema the Earth Lord
30. Amictus the Bug Queen

Beast Quest:
The World of Chaos
31. Komodo the Lizard King
32. Muro the Rat Monster
33. Fang the Bat Fiend
34. Murk the Swamp Man
35. Terra Curse of the Forest
36. Vespick the Wasp Queen

Beast Quest:
The Lost World
37. Convol the Cold-Blooded Brute
38. Hellion the Fiery Foe
39. Krestor the Crushing Terror
40. Madara the Midnight Warrior
41. Ellik the Lightning Horror
42. Carnivora the Winged Scavenger

Beast Quest:
The Pirate King
43. Balisk the Water Snake
44. Koron Jaws of Death
45. Hecton the Body Snatcher
46. Torno the Hurricane Dragon
47. Kronus the Clawed Menace
48. Bloodboar the Buried Doom

Beast Quest:
The Warlock's Staff
49. Ursus the Clawed Roar
50. Minos the Demon Bull
51. Koraka the Winged Assassin
52. Silver the Wild Terror
53. Spikefin the Water King
54. Torpix the Twisting Serpent

Beast Quest:
Master of the Beasts
55. Noctila the Death Owl
56. Shamani the Raging Flame
57. Lustor the Acid Dart
58. Voltrex the Two-Headed Octopus
59. Tecton the Armoured Giant
60. Doomskull the King of Fear

Beast Quest:
The New Age
61. Elko Lord of the Sea
62. Tarrok the Blood Spike
63. Brutus the Hound of Horror
64. Flaymar the Scorched Blaze
65. Serpio the Slithering Shadow
66. Tauron the Pounding Fury

Beast Quest:
The Darkest Hour
67. Solak Scourge of the Sea
68. Kajin the Beast Catcher
69. Issrilla the Creeping Menace
70. Vigrash the Clawed Eagle
71. Mirka the Ice Horse
72. Kama the Faceless Beast

Special Bumper Editions
Vedra & Krimon: Twin Beasts of Avantia
Spiros the Ghost Phoenix
Arax the Soul Stealer
Kragos & Kildor: The Two-Headed Demon
Creta the Winged Terror
Mortaxe the Skeleton Warrior
Ravira, Ruler of the Underworld
Raksha the Mirror Demon
Grashkor the Beast Guard
Ferrok the Iron Soldier

All books priced at £4.99.
Special bumper editions priced at £5.99.

Orchard Books are available from all good bookshops, or can
be ordered from our website: www.orchardbooks.co.uk,
or telephone 01235 827702, or fax 01235 8227703.

Series 7: THE LOST WORLD
Out now!

Can Tom save the chaotic land of Tavania from dark Wizard Malvel's evil plans?

CONVOL
THE COLD-BLOODED BRUTE

978 1 40830 729 8

HELLION
THE FIERY FOE

978 1 40830 730 4

KRESTOR
THE CRUSHING TERROR

978 1 40830 731 1

MADARA
THE MIDNIGHT WARRIOR

978 1 40830 732 8

ELLIK
THE LIGHTNING HORROR

978 1 40830 733 5

CARNIVORA
THE WINGED SCAVENGER

978 1 40830 734 2

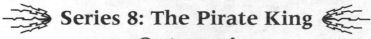